DOLPHIN'S RESCUE
The Story of a Pacific White-Sided Dolphin

SMITHSONIAN OCEANIC COLLECTION

For Monae, a leaper on land and in the water—J.H.

To the memory of a great friend, Michael Parziale—S.J.P.

Published by Soundprints Division of Trudy Corporation, Norwalk, Connecticut.

Series design: Shields & Partners, Westport, CT
Book layout: Marcin D. Pilchowski
Editor: Laura Gates Galvin

First Edition 2005
10 9 8 7 6 5 4 3 2 1
Printed in Singapore

Acknowledgements:
Our very special thanks to Dr. Don E. Wilson of the Department of Systematic Biology at
the Smithsonian Institution's National Museum of Natural History for his curatorial review.
Soundprints would also like to thank Ellen Nanney and Katie Mann at the Smithsonian
Institution's Office of Product Development and Licensing for their help in the creation of this book.
The author would like to thank Dr. John H. Dearborn, who shared the details of the day a
Pacific white-sided dolphin leaped aboard the research ship he was on off the California coast.
The illustrator would like to acknowledge Ben Nussbaum for his direction and dedication to
this project. Thanks to the curators at the Smithsonian for their review of all art and thanks to his
family for their patience and constant support.

*Library of Congress Cataloging-in-Publication Data is
on file with the publisher and the Library of Congress.*

DOLPHIN'S RESCUE
The Story of a Pacific White-Sided Dolphin

by *Janet Halfmann*   Illustrated by *Steven James Petruccio*

Soundprints
Where Children Discover...

4

As dawn breaks off the coast of southern California, a Pacific white-sided dolphin races through the cool waters of the Pacific Ocean. Twenty other dolphins swim through the winter waters with him.

The fast-moving dolphins are chasing a large school of anchovies.

5

Click, click, click. The dolphins send out rapid bursts of sound. The sounds bounce off the thousands of tiny fleeing fish. Dolphin listens to the returning echoes. The echoes tell him where the fish are.

Dolphin and the others circle around the school of fish. They move in closer and closer. They herd the fish into a tight ball.

Noisy gulls squawk in the sky above Dolphin. The flock of gulls will join in the fish feast.

One by one, the dolphins take turns swimming into the school
of fish to eat. Dolphin grabs a beakful of anchovies with his small
pointed teeth. He swallows the fish whole, headfirst, so the spines
won't catch in his throat.

Dolphin makes several passes through the ball of fish.
His stomach is getting full. His group has been hunting
much of the night. Altogether, he has eaten nearly
twenty pounds of fish!

Dolphin hears the sound of a ship's engine nearby and he quickly forgets about eating. When Dolphin was young, he often joined his mother as she rode the waves created by passing ships.

Now a three year old, he is the first in his group to notice the nearby ship. It is a research ship, carrying several scientists. Dolphin leaps from the water as he speeds toward the ship. His tall, hooked dorsal fin throws up a splash of spray behind him. His teammates follow close on his tail.

At the ship, Dolphin claims the best spot. He slides into the big bow wave created by the front of the boat. Some of the other dolphins join him at the bow. Others surf the waves created at the sides and rear of the ship.

As the dolphins surf, long gray stripes stretching down their dark backs catch the sunlight. It looks like the dolphins are wearing suspenders.

Before long, several northern right whale dolphins rush up to the ship. They want to join in the play. The finless black-and-white newcomers look like they are wearing tuxedos. All of the dolphins cruise along, enjoying the almost effortless ride. Only once in a while do they need to beat their tail flukes up and down to swim. The waves created by the boat carry the dolphins along.

While riding the waves, the dolphins frolic and tumble. Dolphin leaps high in the air and turns a complete somersault. He lands on his side with a big smacking splash. The scientists on the ship cheer him on and take pictures.

Dolphin leaps again, straight up into the air. He has never jumped so high before. He clears the ship's bottom rail. He sails past the rail in front of the deckhouse on the second level. He keeps going until he is level with the eyes of the captain standing in the deckhouse.

Dolphin is ten feet above the water!

But this time, Dolphin has jumped so high and so close to the moving ship that he is in trouble. By the time he comes down, the water is no longer below him. Instead, the moving ship has traveled right under him. *Thump!* He flops onto the deck. He almost knocks over two surprised scientists.

At first, Dolphin does not move at all. He just lies quietly. The scientists talk to him softly and stroke his silky skin. They look him over carefully from beak to flukes. The only injury they can find is a small cut near his mouth.

After just a few moments, Dolphin whacks the deck with his tail. Everyone breathes a long sigh of relief. The scientists determine that Dolphin is not badly hurt after all. Now, their main concern is getting him in the water as quickly as possible.

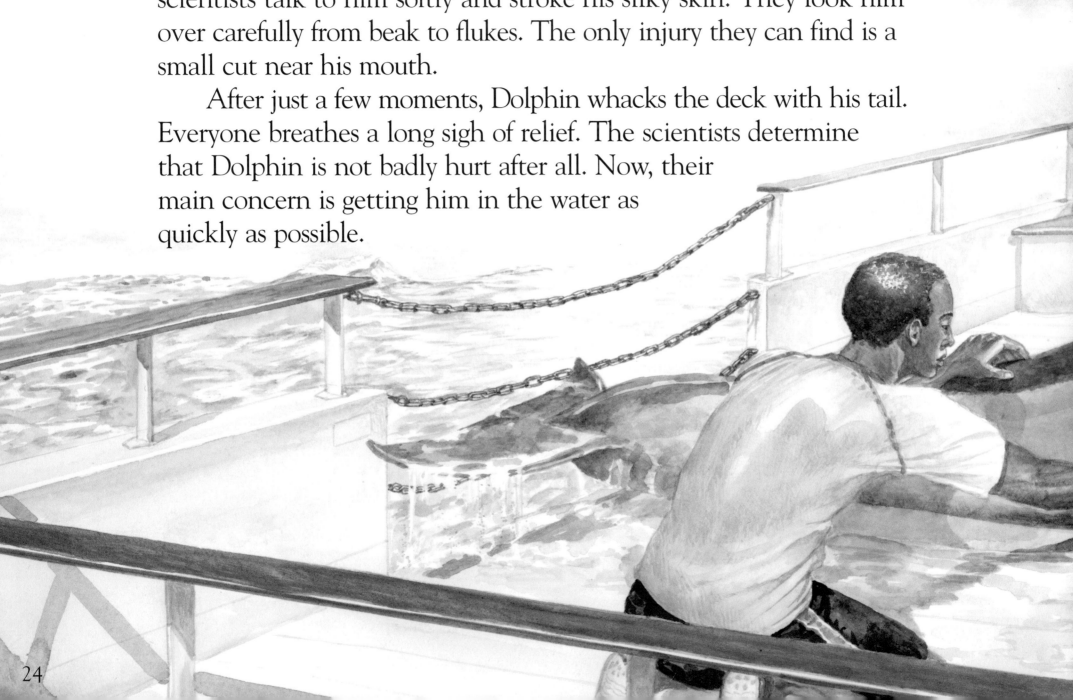

First, the scientists check the ocean waters to make sure no killer whales or other dolphin enemies are near. Then four of the scientists pick up Dolphin in their arms. As gently as they can, they lift him over the side of the ship and back into the ocean.

Dolphin slowly swims away. Two dolphins from his group join him. They swim under him to help him rise to the surface so he can breathe through his blowhole. For a few days, the helpers stay near Dolphin to take care of him.

29

But then one day, Dolphin hears a boat. He is off in a flash, swimming through the water. Soon he is bow riding and leaping once again.

31

About the Pacific White-Sided Dolphin

The Pacific white-sided dolphin is found only in the North Pacific Ocean. The species ranges across a wide band of ocean extending from the coasts of China and Japan to the western coast of North America. These dolphins number about one million in all, with nearly 120,000 off the coast of California. A larger relative, the Atlantic white-sided dolphin, is found in the North Atlantic Ocean.

The Pacific white-sided dolphin measures about 7 to 8 feet long and weighs 165 to 200 pounds. It has a rather stout body, short black beak, large two-tone dorsal fin, and three-part color pattern of black, gray, and white.

Pacific white-sides first mate when they are about 10 years old. The single baby is usually born in summer and is about 3 feet long. The calf nurses for about a year and leaves its mother before two years of age. Pacific white-sided dolphins can live for 45 years.

Pacific white-sided dolphins form large schools, sometimes numbering in the thousands, made up of both sexes and all ages. Group members will care for a dolphin that is injured. The schools often break into smaller groups to fish. They find food by bouncing clicks off schools of fish and squid and analyzing the returning echoes. This is called echolocation. The dolphins also use whistles and other sounds to communicate. Pacific white-sides often seek out the company of other sea animals, especially northern right whale dolphins.

The Pacific white-side is among the most acrobatic of dolphins. It can leap high out of the water, spin, and sometimes turn complete somersaults. It also loves to bow ride. The high leap of the dolphin in this book is based on a true event. In addition to viewing these acrobatic animals in their natural surroundings, you can see them in aquariums, such as the Shedd Aquarium in Chicago, Illinois, and SeaWorld San Antonio in Texas.

Glossary

anchovies: Small, silver fish, related to sardines, that swim in large schools.

beak: The snout or jaws of a dolphin.

blowhole: The nostril on the top of a dolphin's head through which it breathes.

bow ride: To surf or swim in the wave created by the front (bow) of a ship.

dorsal fin: The raised structure on the back of most dolphins.

echoes: Repetitions of sounds caused by sound waves bouncing off a surface.

echolocation: A means of finding objects by sending out sounds and listening to their returning echoes.

flukes: The two flattened halves of a dolphin's tail.

school: A large group of dolphins or fish that swim together.

squid: A sea animal that looks something like an octopus.

Points of Interest in This Book

pp. 8-9: seagulls.
pp. 10-11: anchovies.

pp. 12-13: research ship.
pp. 16-17: northern right whale dolphins.